THE CHAPEL OF HYDRA

CHETAN REDDY KOTHAGADI

Copyright © Chetan Reddy Kothagadi
All Rights Reserved.

This book has been published with all efforts taken to make the material error-free after the consent of the author. However, the author and the publisher do not assume and hereby disclaim any liability to any party for any loss, damage, or disruption caused by errors or omissions, whether such errors or omissions result from negligence, accident, or any other cause.

While every effort has been made to avoid any mistake or omission, this publication is being sold on the condition and understanding that neither the author nor the publishers or printers would be liable in any manner to any person by reason of any mistake or omission in this publication or for any action taken or omitted to be taken or advice rendered or accepted on the basis of this work. For any defect in printing or binding the publishers will be liable only to replace the defective copy by another copy of this work then available.

This book does not really contain any bad habits, it's just made for adventure, drama and creating awareness in people for not doing piracy things. This book is written by the author Chetan Reddy Kothagadi and Co-Author Srivastava Vengala

HAVE FUN AND ENJOY!!!!!!

Contents

Foreword

This story is to all the piracy users and makers, any saying them to stop it

and for the adventurous people who have more anxiety

Preface

I wrote this book because, to say to the world, that not to do anything recklessly and illegally like piracy etc., or else you will lose your life. And I got this idea because nowadays, so many people are doing creating piracy websites, and to stop them, I wrote this book.

Acknowledgements

Author = Chetan Reddy Kothagadi

Co - Author = Srivastava Vengala

Edited By Author And Co-Author

Published By Notion Press

Prologue

This story says that, How four people faced issues by doing piracy things and going to jail and suffering from the cold of that place, after being escaped and the terragon attacks.

Characters

Characters -
  1. STEVE ---------> Journalist
  2. JESSICA -------> Sister of Steve
  3. PETER ---------> Nephew of Steve
  4. FRANK -------> Brother of Steve

CHAPTER ONE

THE PLANNING

It was a bright morning, Jessica and Peter were going to steve's office. Jack was very busy in his office. Jessica and Peter were discussing going on a vacation as most of the city went.

Peter was complaining to Jessica that there is no one to hang out with, but we should go on vacation because I am getting bored. Jessica accepted and said, let's go and ask steve. They saw that steve was very busy in his office.

He was getting non-stop calls from his staff. Then Peter asked "uncle can we go for a vacation, all of my friends went there, there's no one to hang out with". Then Steve says, "No peter, see I have a lot of work to do".

So as steve receives more phone calls, he gets tired and agrees to the vacation. They all decided to go to the place called Costerica forest resort to stay at night.

The Resort is situated in a dense forest called Costerica. Then Steve was sitting on a chair enjoying his sun review on his body.

Jessica was getting irritated by seeing Steve's laziness. Jessica goes near him and by screaming, she says "we came for a vacation to enjoy, not to sit near the sun and enjoy, this we can do it in our home also, that's why let us go home".

Then Steve replies with sadness that 'Ok, it will not repeat again. Then, they went to a shopping mall to buy some accessories, fruits and vegetables for their daily needs. Then, they went to a movie.

But, they did not know that they should not take outside food to the theatre. Then the theatre manager did not allow Steve and Jessica to enter the theatre room.

Then Steve got an idea, as they were professional piracy movie website makers, they started to make a website in Costerica. On the next day, they went to an accessories shop, to buy a camera and all other microphone setups.

Then on the next day, they went to the theatre with accessories, secretly carrying them in the bag and when the manager asked him, they said that they have vegetables and fruits in it, then the manager thought to check their bag, but unfortunately, they found only vegetables and fruits, by the time when the manager was checking Jessica bag, Steve was carrying a bag with all accessories and secretly went without knowing of the manager.

Then, after going to the theatre, they started filming the movie. Then, after filming the movie, they went to their room and started uploading to a fake website called 'punchkala'. Like this, they uploaded so many movies. After some days, FBI officers got to know that, those guys are doing piracy work and taking income from people. Then FBI officers took them to custody and arrested them for 4 years.

But in their hometown, frank was worrying, because, Steve, Peter and Jessica should be reached their hometown in 1 month, but the days passed till 5 months and there was no phone call from steve either Jessica or peter.

CHAPTER TWO

THE NEXT DAY

Frank then decided to go to costerica and search for them. He went to costerica by plane.

There he asked the hotel manager about steve, the manager said that the FBI arrested them for making piracy websites of movies.

Then frank was very worried and was thinking of how to take them out of the jail. The next day, Frank went to the court to get bail for Jessica, Peter and Steve, but he couldn't get the bail papers, he planned to make hen their escape.

Then the next day, Frank asked FBI officers to give a half an hour time to meet steve, peter and Jessica, the officer accepted and gave time to meet, In the meeting, Frank told about his idea to escape the idea was like this "From the backside of the jail, Frank will be with a ladder standing, Peter, Steve and Jessica should wear police uniforms and come out, They should wear the police dresses which were given by frank to them in the meeting.

Then they have to go through the chimney type window which passes through the Jail commissioner officer, then they slowly looked at him and with tiny steps, they walked out of the commissioner room.

Then one police caught them, At the same time steve took a stone and threw it at the police officer, then the police officer fell and they escaped, by the time they are escaping frank was ready with a ladder at the back of the jail and by that, they had escaped.

After they had escaped, they hid in a secret bunker and the news, Steve and Jessica were shown as wanted.

Then they decide to leave the city and go to an island which was routed by frank.

Then they set out to the island in Jessica's helicopter, as the FBI might capture them if they had travelled by car or bus. They reached the island within an hour.

But at the same time, a storm hit the island and the helicopter was not able to land, due to the strong winds of the storm, their helicopter was about to crash, but Jessica gave everyone parachutes and they all jumped from the helicopter before it crashed.

They all were hungry, they ate the food which they brought and built a small shelter for themselves out of wood and bamboo sticks they found on the island.

The night was very cold and they had no blankets to cover themselves, so steve and frank went into the forest to collect some wood so that they could stay warm in the night by lighting the campfire.

For the food, Steve, Jessica and peter went the hunt any animal as to eat, to capture the animals they made a mechanism of steel needle attached to a string, they took a strong spring and attached it to a pipe to make a spear which the animal leads to the unconscious.

They kept the tools ready and kept them at a place so that when the bird struck into it, they could catch it. They waited till the morning, in the morning they woke up, Steve saw a bird stuck to it, immediately he woke up everyone and started for removing the bird from the trap.

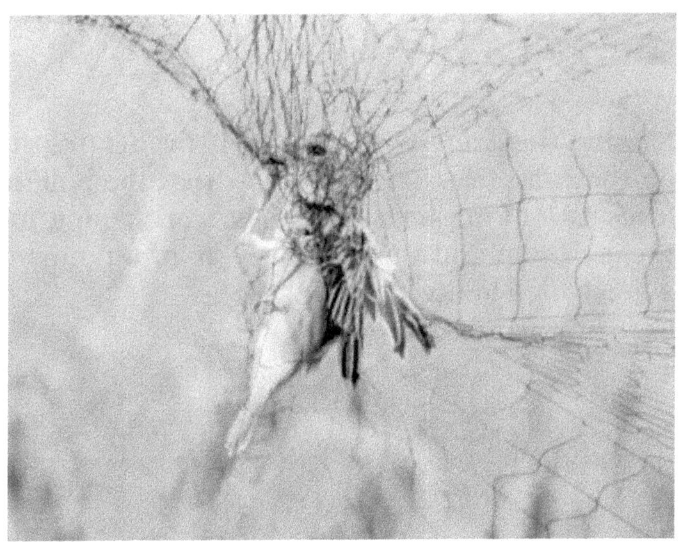

CHAPTER THREE

THE UNKNOWN DESERT

Finally, they removed and ate it by heating it on the campfire. After they saw that the police force is looking for them, they were trying to escape them and they escaped to an unknown place which looks like a desert.

They reached and they were very exhausted, they had nothing except a water bottle. There was only sand and the temperature was very high.

Jessica had an inflatable shelter with her. They stood in the shelter till it was night.

The night was very cold, but as in the morning the sun would be hot they moved on and as they moved they found a small village. They decided to live there for some days.

After some days, even the village has turned into a fireplace, they escaped from there and went to a place which was like a temple full of blood overall and some skulls were lying on the ground.

They were scared of the place, but as there was only a desert, they decided to stay near the temple.

They build temporary shelters around the temple. It was evening by the time they built the shelters. For the campfire, steve and frank collected the twigs which were there nearby the temple. Steve lit the campfire.

They were chit-chatting. Steve started "So what are we going to do here". Jessica replied, " we have to stay here till we find a way".

They were hungry, as it was a desert they couldn't find food, but luckily they found a lake nearby with many fishes in it. They went and captured some fish and cooked and ate them.

It was a very cold night and many scary sounds were coming from the temple. Peter gets scared, so he goes near Jessica and sleeps for the night.

The next morning Steve and frank were searching for a way out in the desert while Jessica and peter stay at the shelter.

Steve and Frank were exhausted due to the hot sun and returned to their shelter. Jessica had already cooked some fish for them, so they all ate and drank some water from the lake and took some rest.

Then as it was cool in the evening frank and steve again went in the search of finding the way out. They did not again find and returned.

CHAPTER FOUR

THE TERRIBLE IDEA THROUGH THE HYDRA

On the next day, Jessica thought to check the north by compass, but she does not have a compass, so she thought to do the Maasai trick. To do the Maasai trick they need to keep a stick in front of the sun and wait for an hour and it shows the way out from the desert.

MAASAI TOOL

Jessica takes some sticks and put's them in the sun. After an hour the stick pointed towards the temple. Everyone get scared as in the night many scary sounds were coming from the temple.

But Steve said "that only that's the way out so we need to do it". Everyone agreed in a nervous manner. They proceed towards the temple and open the door of the temple.

It was dark, so steve lit a stick with fire. They went through the temple and some bats were flying out of the temple, they thought that it was a very dangerous place and by mistakenly frank went missing out from the group and everyone starting looking for frankSteve started Shouting Frank's name loudly, by those sounds some animals started making sounds which were coming from inside the temple.

So, steve did not bother about it and again started shouting then suddenly one dragon came out from the temple everyone got scared and rushed out of the temple but the dragon was not able to come because it was so big and everyone got scared about frank and they did know whether he is dead or still alive that time steve made food by killing a squirrel by taking its meat they started eating. But after eating everyone started crying because frank was lost.

It was night, everyone was depressed that frank was lost, then they all slept but steve was not falling asleep and started making a plan to go in the temple and get out from there. And In the morning, steve discussed his plan with everyone and they accepted the plan of steve.

The plan was to Jessica should go inside and divert the way of the dragon to another side where steve made a jail-like tunnel to capture the dragon.

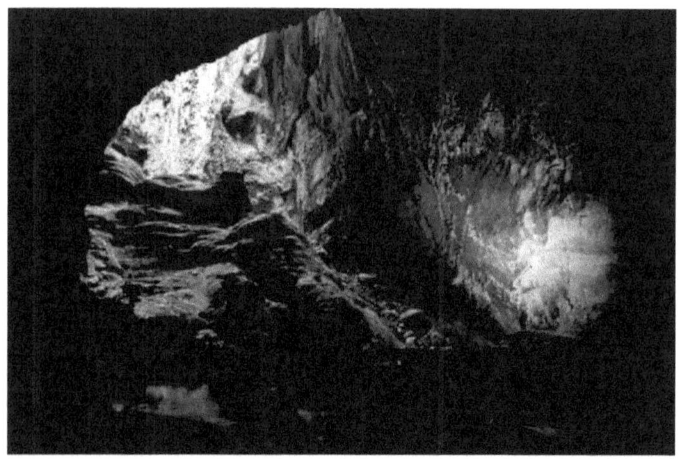

As per the plan, Jessica Tried to divert the dragon, Then the dragon diverted slowly to the cave made by steve, The dragon started to destroy the cave but the cave was so strong then Jessica and other members started to go into the temple deeply then suddenly 7 more dragons came to attack everyone.

Then they hid behind a rock to escape from the dragons. They found a secret narrow passageway through which they escaped. In the passage, they found a shiny rock, so they took it and they also found frank who was in the passageway. They went outside the passageway and found their city. Then everyone discussed that they will surrender to the police as escaping was more dangerous. Steve and Jessica went to surrender to the police.

The police were about to arrest them but when they saw the shiny stone in Jessica's pocket, the police were shocked and congratulated them in honour because they found the stone of the dragon which was very valuable.

So the police said that "U guys have done a very good job, so we are releasing you and we are taking off the piracy case from you guys". As the case was solved steve wanted to know the mystery behind the secret cave so he asked the police for taking the dragons from those and keep them in a special zoo by giving them a shot of B615 by which the dragons can become unconscious.

Then the police can take them from the temple to keep in the special zoo and after clearing the temple steve went through the temple so he found a mysterious room in which there is a lot of painting of one king called Jamkeshwara Siddha and there is a book of him of his whole time story.

In that story it was written that the dragons are his pets and was taking care of him as the dragons had saved his life from the enemy called Hurshada Masuliya.

Who was trying to steal the shiny stone of Jamkeshwara Siddha so that he could rule the world?

Then Jamkeshwara sent his 2 dragons to kill Hurshuda. Then he died and Jamkeshwara ordered his dragons to save the shiny stone.

After some years Jamkeshwara breathed his last, and from then the dragons were protecting the stone.

Then the temple was made as a tourist spot and steve was doing his daily chores and was writing articles in his office.

MYSTERY OF
THE GOLDEN
CAVE

CHETAN REDDY
KOTHAGADI

Enter Caption

Enter Caption

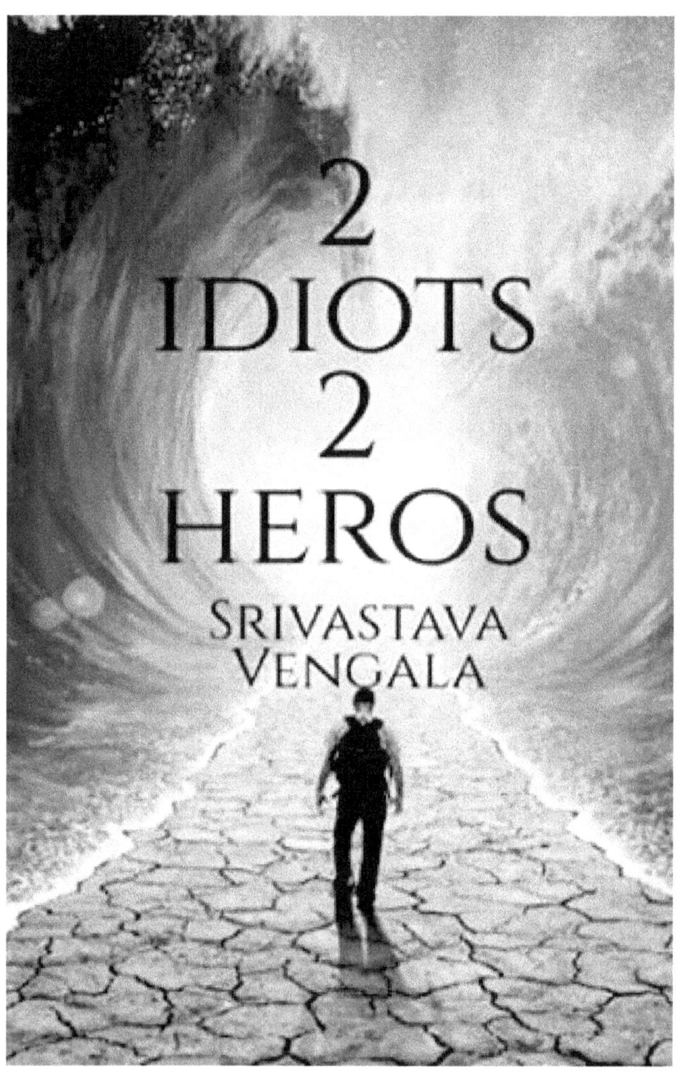

Enter Caption

Enter Caption

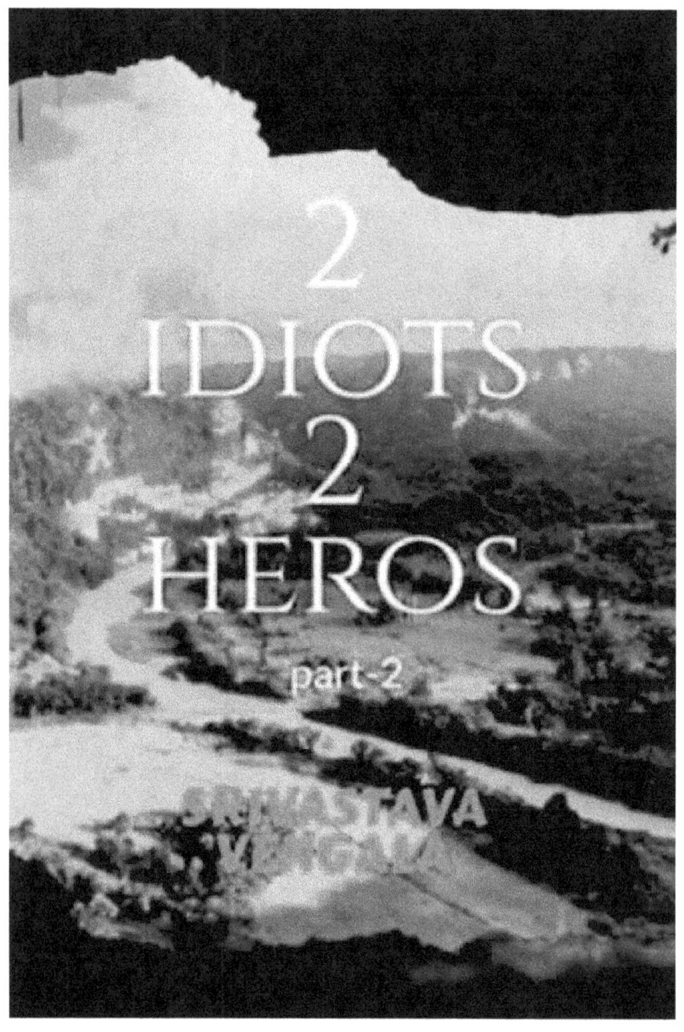

Enter Caption

Your Opinion Matters

Write your opinion in this google docs link =

https://bit.ly/3pGnBsp

Enter Caption

* 9 7 9 8 8 8 8 6 2 9 4 4 2 2 *